Usborne Farmyard Tales

# THE OLD STEAM TRAIN

## Heather Amery
## Illustrated by Stephen Cartwright

Edited by Jenny Tyler
Language Consultant: Betty Root

There is a little yellow duck to find on every page.

# This is Apple Tree Farm.

This is Mrs. Boot, the farmer. She has two children, called Poppy and Sam, and a dog called Rusty.

"Hurry up," says Mrs. Boot.

"Where are we going today?" asks Poppy.
"To the old station," says Mrs. Boot.

They walk down the lane.

"Why are we going? There aren't any trains," says Sam. "Just you wait and see," says Mrs. Boot.

"What's everyone doing?" asks Poppy.

"They're cleaning up the old station," says
Mrs. Boot. "Everyone's helping today."

"There's lots to do."

"Poppy and Sam can help me," says the painter.
"Coats off and down to work," says Mrs. Boot.

Poppy and Sam work hard.

Sam brings pots of paint and Poppy brings the
brushes. Mrs. Boot sweeps the platform.

"What's that noise?"

"It's the train. It's coming," says Mrs. Boot. "Look, it's a steam train," says Poppy. "How exciting."

The train puffs down the track.

It stops at the platform. The engine gives a long whistle. Everyone cheers and waves.

"Look, there's Dad," says Sam.

"He's helping the train driver, just for today,"
says Mrs. Boot. "Isn't he lucky?" says Poppy.

"All aboard," says Mrs. Boot.

"I'll get on here," says Poppy. "Come on, Rusty," says Sam. "I'll shut the door," says Mrs. Boot.

"Where are you going?"

"Aren't you coming with us?" asks Sam. "You stay on the train," says Mrs. Boot. "I'll be back soon."

"Look, there she is."

"She's wearing a cap," says Poppy. "Yes, I'm the guard just for today," says Mrs. Boot.

Mrs. Boot waves a flag.

The train whistles and starts to puff away. Mrs. Boot jumps on the train and shuts the door.

"We're off," says Sam.

The train chugs slowly down the track. "Doesn't the old station look good now?" says Poppy.

# "I like steam trains," says Sam.

# "The station is open again," says Mrs. Boot. "And we can ride on the steam train every weekend."

First published in 1999 by Usborne Publishing Ltd., Usborne House, 83-85 Saffron Hill, London EC1N 8RT, England. www.usborne.com
Copyright © 1999 Usborne Publishing Ltd.